Eli & The Moonday

written by Ashton Smith
& illustrated by Scott L. Smith, Jr.

Eli & The Moonday
written by Ashton Smith
illustrated by Scott L. Smith, Jr.
Copyright © 2021 Holy Water Books

ISBN-13: 978-1-950782-30-7
All rights reserved.
Holy Water Books (Publisher)

HOLYWATERBOOKS

please check out our
other titles online at
www.holywaterbooks.com

Dedicated to our wolfcub, Eli,
who did indeed discover Moonday,
and with whom everyday reveals
new worlds of imagination.

And to Mama Mary,
Who said "Yes" for us all
And reflects the light of her Son.

"A great sign appeared in the sky, a woman
clothed with the sun, with the moon under her
feet, and on her head a crown of twelve stars."
Revelation 12:1

Eli

& The

Moonday

"Mama, is it almost 'Moonday'?" asked Eli, but Mama couldn't understand with the broom in her hand and the spoon for stirring the dinner in the other. She said, "It's Tuesday."

"No, Mama," persisted Eli. "Moonday." But Eli got distracted by the fuzzy wolf hood laying on the piano. He grabbed it up and pulled in on his head and ran off howling as four-year-olds do.

It was dinner time, then bath time, and then prayer time. And after prayer Mama tucked him tightly into bed. There was a cold front moving in so the covers needed to be right.

"Mama, is it Moonday?" asked Eli.

Mama thought for a moment and brushed the hair on his forehead with her hand. "It's the best kind of 'Moonday'," she said leaning in towards his ear, and her voice had the mystery that Eli loved. There was a kiss, and Mama left a crack in the door for the light to come in.

But Eli was too excited to sleep, and the glow was too bright behind the blinds. He needed just a peek. He grabbed his treasure pail from under the bed.

He tiptoed to the window and pulled back the blinds.

There was a full moon and it was as large as a planet in the sky. The glow spilled into a creamy staircase that led right to his bedroom window.

It was the most marvelous Moonday Eli had ever seen. He hoisted up the window and stepped out.

It was bright and dark and
cold and warm, and Eli
wanted to chase the moon.
So he mounted the
moonlight stairs.
He could hear
Mama playing
Beethoven at the
piano and it was loud,
then softer, softer.

And Eli got higher, higher until he
was quite above the house and
quite brave, too.

The cold was tickling his toes, but such things don't matter when you dance on the moonlight stairs. Moondays were the best days. And moondancing was a privilege.

The higher he stepped the bouncier his dance became until his toes rarely touched the stairs at all.

And the stars grew happy just watching him.
They congratulated him on his dancing
excellence and blinked rapidly in applause. Eli
was quite close now and could see the Moon's
big smile. He howled as four-year-olds often
do and took a great giant leap and landed on
the moon.

Oh, how dancey he felt!
And how delicious was
the moonlight beneath his feet!
He shoved some into
his treasure pail
to bring to Mama.
He thought he could
still hear her in the distance
playing Beethoven
on the piano.

The moon was a magnificent landscape
of creamy gullies and hills.
Eli ran them over with his chilly feet
and somersaulted in the valleys.

Eli climbed the moon mountains and
it didn't matter if he fell because he
always landed softly.

He visited the moon wolves who lived there and when he pet them their tongues hung out lazily. Eli was a special friend of wolf-kin and joined them in their howling, which was answered by small yelps from their cubs from earth below. And they ran alongside him as he danced, jumping and panting.

The wax-faced Moonmen gave Eli a parade! Eli was cheered through moonbrick streets and was sung to once and again as it echoed back.

There was quite a fuss made of him and he was given a castle of his own, made of mooncheese, and he reveled in the excitement of exploring the secret passages.

But alas, Eli ate monstrous amounts of mooncheese, which made him very sleepy and think of his bed with the covers just right.

So he climbed the High Mountain of the Moonday Queen who was white with twelve stars shining above her head.

And he clung to her as they flew
through the farewells of Moonmen
and the gullies and hills and through
the stars.

Moonday Queen's feathers were
soft and safe and familiar, and Eli
rested his head through
cottoned-clouds, past mountain
summits, and frozen forests.

Finally, the Moonday Queen brought him into sight of something familiar ...,

It was home but it was covered in white now.

Eli loved Snowday!

Mama was still playing Moonlight Sonata.

The piano music was loud now, but Eli was sleepy.

The music was a lullaby as Moonday Queen swooped down past the big oak tree by Eli's bedroom and flew through his window.

Eli yawned and sleepily waved goodbye to Moonday Queen as he climbed into bed.

Mama stopped playing the piano but Eli was already asleep and Moonday Queen was nearly back on her perch on High Mountain.

Mama slipped through the crack in Eli's bedroom door and closed his window. She piled an extra blanket on top of Eli, and took his pail of moonlight, which was spilling onto the floor, and put it on his bedside table for his nightlight.

Mama brushed the hair on his forehead with her hand, kissed him and closed the door behind her.

"Moon-night."